Magic Pony

The Lucky Bunny

Annie looked up and cried out with delight. Ned, the pony in the poster, was alive again. He leaned from her bedroom window as if over a stable door. She quickly looked around to make sure no one else was witnessing this extraordinary sight.

"Ned, I'm so glad to see you. I've been waiting for you to come back."

**Join Annie on all her adventures
with Ned, the Magic Pony!**

Magic Pony
The Lucky Bunny

Elizabeth Lindsay

Illustrated by John Eastwood

A
LITTLE APPLE
PAPERBACK

SCHOLASTIC INC.

New York Toronto London Auckland Sydney
Mexico City New Delhi Hong Kong Buenos Aires

For Jessamy, with love

ISBN 0-439-56007-1
Text copyright © 1997 Elizabeth Lindsay.
Illustrations copyright © 1997 John Eastwood.

All rights reserved. Published by Scholastic Inc., 557 Broadway, New York, NY 10012, by arrangement with Scholastic Children's Books, Scholastic Ltd. SCHOLASTIC, Little Apple, and associated logos are trademarks and/or registered trademarks of Scholastic Inc.

12 11 10 9 8 7 6 5 4 3 2 1   4 5 6 7 8 9/0

Printed in the U.S.A.   40
First Scholastic printing, May 2004

Chapter 1

Visitors

Annie lay stretched out on her bed, hands behind her head, with her tabby cat, Tabitha, a purring ball on her chest. Drifting into a wonderful dream, Annie imagined Ned, the chestnut pony in the poster on her wall, jumping from his picture.

"Take me on an adventure, Ned," she

said, climbing onto his strong back. "Like you did before!" With a whoosh and whirl of magic wind, they are in the field on the other side of the road. Here, Penelope Potter's pony, Pebbles, watches in astonishment as they soar over a line of blue barrels, the very same barrels Pebbles jumps so often with his owner. And Annie doesn't wobble once, because in a dream everything goes according to plan and she never ever falls off.

There was a big sigh and Annie

opened her eyes, gently toppling Tabitha onto the covers before sitting up. Tabby curled up in the warm space Annie had left behind and promptly fell asleep. Annie swung her feet to the floor, gazed at Ned's poster, and sighed another sigh, one of loss and longing.

It seemed like forever since she had bought the pony poster

at Cosby's Magic Emporium. A long, chestnut hair from Ned's tail hung on the wall above her bed. The hair wasn't pretend, it was real, and Annie knew in her heart of hearts that Ned would come out of the poster again — the magic had always worked when Annie needed to see Ned. Maybe, if she wished hard enough, and talked to Ned while he was still in his poster, she would make the magic happen.

She stood up to touch the cool, shiny paper and ran a finger along Ned's white blaze on his forehead.

"Are you going to come to life again? Are you?" she asked, but nothing changed and there was not the slightest hint that Ned was anything other than a pony in a poster.

Annie turned to her three china

horses on the windowsill. Esmerelda had her back to Prince and Percy. Annie rearranged them into a nose-to-nose huddle so they could talk to one another, unaware that the head in the poster had turned, just a little, to follow what she was doing.

"Esmerelda, Prince, Percy — I'm going

on an adventure. Tell Ned to come, too."
But the three china horses were silent.

It was no good. She would have to
have an adventure on her own. Annie
grabbed an invisible rein, jumped onto a
chestnut pony who wasn't there, and set
off at a canter to the top of the stairs.
Then clumpity, clumpity, clumpity all
the way down to the bottom, riding like
the wind. Her thumping feet brought
Mom hurrying from the living room.

"Annie, that's an awful lot of noise. I
thought you'd fallen downstairs." Annie
jogged on the spot, her pony prancing. "If

you've got nothing better to do, Jamie's outside and might like some help. He's going to make Fred disappear."

Annie shook her head. "He'll never do it."

"I have my doubts, too," Mom admitted. "But he insists on trying. Why don't you give him a hand?"

It was true that Jamie's conjuring was getting better and his latest card trick was awesome. But he didn't stand a chance of making a goldfish vanish, let alone a goldfish in a bowl. No, she had better things to do than get involved with that.

"I'll just say hello to Pebbles," Annie said and, cantering to the front door, she reared up to undo the latch. "And Penelope, if she's there." Mom smiled and left her to it.

Annie trotted down the garden path to the front gate. Ned would jump it with an easy leap and a swish of his tail. If she tried it by herself, common sense said that she would end up flat on her face. If only Ned would come out of his poster!

Reaching the other side of the road, Annie reined in her invisible pony and dismounted. She put her foot on the middle rung of the field gate, hoisted herself up, and leaned over. She was just in time to see Penelope lead Pebbles out of the far gate to his stable. Annie swung herself to the other side and, landing on her invisible pony's back, set off at a gallop across the well-cut grass.

"Whoa, boy, whoa," she said, arriving at the far gate. Breathing hard, she let herself into the small stable yard and set her pretend pony free.

"Hello, Penelope. Need any help?"

Penelope, who was tying Pebbles's halter rope to the ring outside his stable, considered the offer.

"You can groom him if you like. You can't ride him, though. My cousin Daisy's going to do that. I'm getting him ready for her."

"Your cousin?" Annie inquired, eager to get her hands on a brush before Penelope changed her mind.

"Daisy, Auntie Peg, and Uncle Ralph are staying for the weekend. They're back at the house. I've come over to get Pebbles ready. Daisy's younger than me, so I'm looking after her."

"That's nice," said Annie, getting Pebbles's red-bristled brush ready to start.

Penelope held up the pony's yellow-stained tail and wrinkled her nose. "It'll have to be washed, Pebbles. Daisy can't ride you with a tail like that."

"Not a good idea," agreed Annie

happily, for if Penelope was busy tail-washing, it meant she could brush away to her heart's content. She began at once on the pony's dappled gray neck. Pebbles stood like a rock with his eyes half closed.

He was particularly itchy around the ears and when Annie scratched them, he leaned into her hand and wobbled his

bottom lip. She scratched harder. Wobble, wobble, wobble went the lip. In the end, Annie's fingers ached so much she had to stop, and Pebbles breathed a sigh of regret.

She brushed his neck, his back, his tummy, his front and rear legs — and that was just one side. By the time Penelope arrived with a bucket of hot water, Annie was dust-covered and tired.

"Not bad," said Penelope. "You've

missed a little there, though — and don't forget to comb his mane."

Annie nearly said, *And who made you queen?* but stopped herself. She didn't want to argue with Penelope, not when she was about to be allowed to comb Pebbles's mane. She changed sides and brushed and brushed while Penelope plunged the dirty tail into the hot water.

Pebbles was quite used to all this and continued dozing, not minding at all when Penelope squeezed on a large dollop of horse shampoo and got down to a thorough rubbing. Soon his tail was a mass of dirty brown foam.

"Fill a bucket, Annie. I need to rinse it."

Annie put down the brush and surveyed her work. Only the mane to do. But first, Madam Penelope wanted water.

Honestly! Hadn't she heard of the word *please*?

Annie staggered back from the faucet with a bucketful, only to be told to get another.

"I need lots," said Penelope. "To get all the soap out."

Dutifully, Annie filled another bucket.

She was about to rummage around in the grooming box for the mane comb when a car drove down Penelope's driveway across the road and into the little yard.

"Here they are," cried Penelope, whirling the dripping tail around and around and showering Annie.

"Hey, do you mind!"

"Annie, get rid of the buckets," Penelope ordered, thrusting two at her. "I'll quickly do his mane."

"But I was going to do that!"

Penelope ignored her.

Fed up, Annie dumped the buckets in the tack room. There wasn't much point in hanging around only to be in the way, so she started walking toward the gate.

A girl with a mass of blond curls, wearing a new pair of jodhpurs and gleaming riding boots, climbed out of the car. *Must be Daisy*, thought Annie, and she watched from the top of the gate, envying the little girl's brand-new riding clothes. The man — Uncle Ralph, Annie

supposed — opened the back of the car and revealed a brown hutch.

"Get the other end, Daisy."

"It's too heavy by myself," said Daisy.

Penelope glanced at Annie. Annie took the hint.

"I'll help," she said, jumping from her perch.

Daisy and Annie got one end and Uncle Ralph the other and, between

them, they lifted out the hutch. They were about to place it on the concrete when the hutch door swung open.

"Careful, Floppy will get out," said Daisy.

But, Annie realized on closer inspection, whoever or whatever Floppy was, it had already gotten out, because the hutch was empty.

Chapter 2

The Face at the Window

Annie quickly learned that Floppy was Daisy's pet rabbit. The most perfect, snow-white creature in the whole world, with a name to match his ears.

"They flop sideways," Daisy said with a sob, twisting Floppy's red leash in her hands. "And his paws are pink and his nose is pink and it twitches. You'll know

22

him the moment you see him." But since Floppy appeared to be lost forever, Daisy's sobs became heartbroken wails.

Daisy and her parents had arrived late yesterday evening, Annie was told. It had been too dark to find a place out-of-doors for Floppy to spend the night, so they had left him in the back of the car, locked in his hutch — or so they thought. Uncle Ralph had left a gap in the back door to make sure Floppy had plenty of fresh air. But now, when they wanted to take him for a walk in Pebbles's field, he was gone, already walking himself goodness-knows-where.

Penelope clasped her hands over her ears, trying to cut out Daisy's agonizing cries.

"I'll look for him," said Annie, understanding that if Floppy were her pet

23

rabbit, she would be feeling just like Daisy.

"Look anywhere you like," said Penelope. "But a rabbit on its own all night in our yard will certainly have been eaten by the fox."

Daisy's cries instantly became worse, and Uncle Ralph looked even more worried. Annie thought it was best not to mention that Tabitha had also been known to bring home the occasional rabbit. Instead, she tried to be comforting.

"He may have found a nice little hole to hide in. He may have gone visiting and met up with other rabbits." At this crumb of hope, Daisy's wails lessened.

"Do you think so?" she asked between sobs.

"It's possible."

Uncle Ralph sent Annie a grateful look.

"Anyway," said Annie. "I'll get going. I'll look in the streets, in Mrs. Plumley's front yard, in ours, and in the woods."

"Where will *we* look, Penelope?" Daisy asked, looking brighter now that positive action was being taken.

"Our yard and the field, I suppose." Penelope sighed. "Both are huge. It'll take forever."

Annie waved good-bye. She'd start her search right away. She hurried past Uncle Ralph's shiny car and, once out of sight, jumped up on her invisible pony and trotted into the road. She looked this way and that. No white rabbit was to be seen.

Turning toward home, Annie reached the next-door neighbor's house first. She peered over the gate. Nothing on the grass. Not a glimmer of white fur among Mrs. Plumley's prize dahlias or behind the willowy hollyhocks. At the next gate, her own, a soft burbling sound, the sort horses make by blowing through their noses, brought her to an abrupt stop.

"Hello, down there!"

Annie looked up and cried out with delight. Ned, the pony in her poster, was alive again. He leaned out from her bedroom window as if he were over a stable door. She quickly looked around to make sure no one else was looking at this extraordinary sight.

"Ned, I'm so glad to see you. I've been wanting you to come back forever."

"Well, here I am," said the pony, and promptly disappeared.

It wasn't until Annie saw a branch sway on the fig tree growing by the wall that she saw him again. Now as tiny as Percy, the smallest of her china horses, Ned sprang from leaf to leaf, all the way down the tree, until he balanced on the same level as her nose.

"Help me down, and we'll go for a ride." His little voice reminded her of tinkling bells.

"A ride! Oh, Ned, I'd love to, but I'm looking for a lost rabbit."

"A lost rabbit, huh? I'll help you look."

With glowing eyes, Annie held out her hands, palms flat, for Ned to climb

onto, then carefully lowered him to the ground. In the time it takes to blink, he was at her side, big and strong, the size

Pebbles had been when she'd groomed him, wearing a bridle and a saddle, ready for her to mount.

Annie took hold of the reins and swung herself up on his back. The moment her seat touched the saddle, her sweatshirt, jeans, and sneakers disappeared. In their place was a riding jacket, jodhpurs, and brown boots; underneath the jacket, a shirt and tie. Her hands wore pale riding gloves, and on her head was a velvet helmet.

"I love these riding clothes! I always look like I'm Penelope Potter going to a horse show!" she exclaimed.

"You do indeed," said Ned, and he pulled the gate open with his teeth and went into the road. "Now, where shall we look?"

"In Winchway Wood. It's this way. Turn left." Ned did so. "The rabbit's named Floppy and he's completely white. He escaped in Penelope's yard."

Ned snorted and his trotting feet made delicate clicks on the road's hard surface, but unlike Pebbles, he wore no shoes. It was strange not to hear the ring of metal.

Annie did her best up-down, up-down rising trot until they reached the path that led into the woods where the road ended.

"Be careful, Ned. Lots of people walk their dogs this way. We mustn't be seen!"

"Don't worry. Just say hello and on we'll go."

"But you're a secret!"

"Where I come from is a secret. That you and I can become tiny is a secret. When we're ordinary size like this, it doesn't matter, as long as no one recognizes who you are."

"Are you sure it will work again?"

"When you are dressed like that, you have the perfect disguise. And, of course, I will never speak when someone is near!" Ned's confidence in the riding clothes as a disguise made Annie long to look at herself in the mirror. She pulled her chin strap straight and sat tall, feeling like a different person.

"Hold on tight," said Ned. "And keep a lookout for that bunny."

Annie twisted some mane around her fingers, just in case, and Ned broke into a canter. To her delight, Annie found she hardly wobbled at all.

"You've really gotten better," cried Ned. "I told you I'd teach you to ride. Do you remember?" Annie did remember. "Don't you worry about a thing. Relax and it's as easy as breathing. You can leave the steering to me."

Annie did just that, enjoying herself while her eyes darted here and there, looking for the white rabbit. Ned cantered beneath the stately beech trees, his hooves beating out a steady rhythm on the path. A log lay ahead and Annie knew he was going to jump it.

"Don't worry, just like last time, you'll

hardly notice we've left the ground," Ned cried. The log came closer, and the nearer they got the bigger it looked, but Ned didn't shy from it. They flew over the log, and Annie stayed on, even when they thudded to the ground on the other side. A bubble of laughter burst from her. Jumping was always fun. Now Ned

galloped, ears flat back, his mane flying, while the wind forced tears from Annie's eyes and whistled in her ears.

Suddenly, there was a dog, small and white, barking ferociously. It came at them without warning. Ned shied off the path, made a whiplash turn, and raised a forefoot, ready to confront the foe. Annie landed halfway up his neck.

"It's Ruddles." She gasped, barely clinging on. "Sit, Ruddles! Sit and stay!"

The little dog stopped, cocked his head on one side, and sat, wondering how this stranger knew his name. Annie hauled herself back into the saddle. "Ruddles lives next door." The little dog raised an ear and waited expectantly.

"Mrs. Plumley must be taking him for a walk. Look, here she comes."

Stout Mrs. Plumley waddled down the path toward them, waving Ruddles's leash.

"Ruddles! Come here, you little varmint," she called. "You leave that pony alone."

"Let's go, Ned," said Annie. "If she recognizes me, she'll certainly tell Mom, and then I'll have to explain everything."

"Just like all the other times, you have the perfect disguise," said Ned. "It'll work this time, too. But remember, if you get off, don't let go of the reins or the riding clothes will vanish."

Annie crossed her fingers and wished for luck. She hoped it would work like it did last time.

"Good dog, Ruddles. Good boy," said

Mrs. Plumley, puffing and stooping to clip on the leash. She smiled up at Annie. "Sorry about his barking, dear. He's a little noisy, but he doesn't mean any harm." Annie smiled back but didn't say anything. "You've got a pretty pony there. A lovely chestnut color. What's his name?"

Annie swallowed nervously.

"Ned."

"What's that you say?" Mrs. Plumley tipped her head to one side and waited.

"His name is Ned!"

"Ned is very handsome," said Mrs. Plumley, patting Ned's sleek neck. "Well, I must be going. Come along, Ruddles. Enjoy your ride, my dear."

"Thank you," said Annie. "I will." And she breathed a huge sigh of relief as Mrs. Plumley pulled the reluctant Ruddles on down the path.

"There," said Ned. "It's just like I said."

"It is," said Annie, grinning hugely. "The disguise worked again."

Ned raised his head and stepped out in a businesslike way.

"Let's keep looking," he said. "We've got a white rabbit to find."

Chapter 3

Rabbit Search

Ned trotted between the trees, twisting around the solid trunks. Annie scanned the ground at either side while Ned kept a forward lookout. From grassy patches, the gray, wood-dwelling rabbits hurried and scurried, flashing cottony white tails as they hopped down holes and disappeared between tree roots. But a snow-white rabbit with pink nose and paws was nowhere to be seen. With all their looking here and there, Annie and Ned could only reach one conclusion — Floppy was not in Winchway Wood.

"Well, you can't say we haven't looked," said Annie. "We must have covered every bump, dip, nook, and cranny."

"We certainly have." Ned came to a stop and blew a burbling pony sigh. "It's been a good ride, but I say we go home."

Ned turned down the path, and Annie was filled with sadness. She loved being on Ned's strong back; he was a real friend. But she was concerned for Floppy.

"I hope Penelope was wrong when she said a night outside for Floppy meant the fox would get him."

Ned blew again, pursuing a thought.

"He's found somewhere more rabbit-friendly, that's all." And he stretched his long neck.

"What's more rabbit-friendly than woods full of rabbits?" wondered Annie.

"A garden full of cabbage, lettuce, and juicy peas!"

"Of course!" said Annie. "Grass must be boring for a rabbit that's used to treats. I bet Daisy gives him lots."

"I'm sure she does," agreed Ned.

"Like Mrs. Plumley gives Pebbles a carrot every day. He likes it so much he waits by the gate."

"See what I mean?"

"Well," said Annie, "the nearest place to Penelope's yard where a rabbit can find all those treats is our vegetable garden."

"Mmm! Better take a look," said Ned.

"But he can't get in. Dad knows all about rabbits. There's fencing around the whole garden." Annie frowned. "I keep thinking that he might have gone the

other way, to the main road, and gotten squashed by a car. That would be terrible."

"It certainly would be," agreed Ned, trotting forward. "The sooner we find out what's happened to him, the better. We'll search your garden next."

They reached the path, and ahead of them lay the log. Ned cantered toward it. His jump was effortless, although his rider slipped sideways. He stopped so Annie could straighten up.

"It was going downhill," she said, excusing herself and adjusting her hat.

"You're doing very well, very well."

They continued along the path and out of the woods, reaching Annie's house in a matter of minutes.

"We'd better go around by the side gate," she said, dismounting. "There's less chance of bumping into anyone." Keeping hold of the reins, she twisted

around to admire her brand-new jodhpurs and shiny riding boots.

"It would be best if you carry me," said Ned.

Annie knew her wonderful clothes would disappear the moment she let go. She closed her eyes . . .

"One, two, three!" She dropped the reins. When she opened her eyes again, Ned and the riding clothes had disappeared and she was back in her grubby jeans, sweatshirt, and boring old sneakers. But she brightened up when the tiny Ned trotted around her toes and she bent down with both hands outstretched. He

jumped neatly onto her palms, and she lifted him carefully. Keeping her hands steady, Annie pushed the gate open with her bottom and slipped down the path toward the vegetable garden.

The first person she saw was Jamie. His magician's gear was spread every which way across the grass, and he was balancing his top hat on a finger and holding up his magic wand. The goldfish bowl was sitting on the little table from the living room and Fred, their goldfish, was fluttering his fins and staring out at the flowers.

"Abracadabra, vroom, vroom, vanish!"

Jamie spun the hat onto his head and twirled his cloak. Fred, bowl, and table were enveloped behind his cloak while Jamie began to struggle awkwardly.

"Annie, if you'll be my assistant, I can do it," said Jamie, catching sight of her.

"Do what?" Annie asked, although she knew the answer.

"Make Fred disappear. I can't do it on my own because of the water. Every time I try, I tip the bowl." He uncovered the goldfish, who was swimming around and around frantically.

"Poor Fred, you're scaring him," said Annie. "Anyway, that's cheating. It's not magic if you've got to get someone else to do it for you."

"Of course it's not cheating. Doing magic is sleight of hand, illusion, and stuff like that. An assistant just helps. What have you got there?"

Annie had been talking to Jamie with her hands held out.

"Oh, nothing." And, indeed, when she looked, there was nothing. She shook them out to show this was true and at the same time glanced around. Much to her surprise it was Ned who'd vanished, although Annie knew it had nothing to do with Jamie's magic tricks. Ned was hiding.

Suddenly, there was a bang, crash, and yelp in the shed, and Dad danced into the yard holding his thumb. Annie rushed to see what was the matter, along with Mom, who ran out from the kitchen.

"What's happened?" they both asked. Dad puffed and groaned and, in an effort not to yell again, got red in the face.

"I think it's his thumb," said Annie.

"Must have hit it with the hammer," said Jamie.

Dad let out another groan. "You could say that!"

"That's too bad," said Mom, gently lifting his hand to look. "Better run cold water on it to stop the bruising."

Annie leaned her face against Dad's

arm. "Poor Dad. I hope it doesn't hurt too much."

"At least your thumb's still there," said Jamie cheerily.

Dad ignored that remark and went indoors.

"Okay, you two, it's lunchtime," said Mom. "Stop what you're doing and come in. And don't leave that fish outside where the cat can get it."

"Annie, can you carry Fred?" Jamie asked, dropping his cloak and hat in a pile and offering the bowl expectantly.

"Why can't you?" grumbled Annie.

"I need two hands for the table."

Annie took the bowl, taking care not to slop any water, and peered at Fred. He seemed calmer now that he'd stopped being shaken around, and he peered back.

Having to go in for lunch was a real nuisance. Annie wanted to find Ned and look for Floppy. Annoyed, she followed Jamie and the table indoors.

Annie was glad to get Fred safely back in his place on the bookshelf and, while Mom came in with a plate of sandwiches, she quickly looked out the window. She hoped that Ned, wherever he was, realized she had been dragged in for lunch.

Mom returned to the kitchen to get drinks for everyone.

"Annie, there's a cake on the counter. Come and get it for me, will you?"

Having gotten as far as the kitchen, Annie was tempted to sneak outside but when she saw that the cake was a yummy chocolate one, she carried it into the dining room.

"When did you make this?" she asked.

"I didn't. Mrs. Plumley did. It's a thank-

you for keeping an eye on things while she's away."

"But she's not away."

"She will be tomorrow. She and Ruddles are going to town to stay with her sister for a few days."

"After lunch I'll cut her a couple of heads of lettuce and pull some carrots for her to take," said Dad.

"She'd appreciate that." Mom nodded. "Carrots you buy never taste as good as the homegrown ones. Plates, Annie. Pass Dad a sandwich, Jamie." Annie gave Dad a plate, and Jamie obediently offered the sandwiches.

"Wow, your thumb's getting really red. I bet the nail comes off."

"Don't sound so excited," said Dad.

"What were you doing, anyway?" Mom asked.

"There's a hole to fix. Some animal pushed its way through the fence."

A hole in the fence! Annie's mind raced. Did that mean that Floppy was in the garden after all? She wished Mom would hurry and cut the cake. She wanted to go and look.

"Now, Jamie, tell me . . ." asked Mom, sipping her tea and taking forever to get to the point. Annie fiddled impatiently with a sandwich. "Did you made Fred disappear?"

Jamie's face took on a look of despair.

"I need a rabbit. You can't do magic tricks with a goldfish. The water tips out. Every magician should have a rabbit."

"And white doves," added Annie. "To pull out from sleeves and top hats."

"Don't encourage him," said Mom. "A cat and a goldfish are plenty of pets for one family."

"Don't even think of a rabbit," Dad

joined in. "Garden pests, that's what they are." Annie fidgeted in her chair, aware that Floppy might be a garden pest right now. Jamie scowled with disappointment.

At last, Mom slid a knife through the gooey chocolate cake.

"Pass your plate, Annie."

Annie bit into the dark stickiness, lumpy with chocolate chips and gooey with chocolate cream icing. It was bliss. She was chewing quickly on the last mouthful when a loud whinny from the garden startled her into action. Ignoring the protests from Mom and Dad, she swallowed, plopped down her plate, and ran.

It was Ned calling. She had to go.

Chapter 4

The Thief in the Garden

Annie charged out the back door and raced down the path. Was she looking for a big Ned or a little Ned? She didn't know. When she got to the shed, she found big Ned behind it, tacked up and waiting. She knew what to do. She reached for his withers and vaulted.

"Well done," said the pony, and the

moment she was astride, a wild wind spun them away, leaving his voice an echo. When it was calm again, it seemed as if they were in a different place. The wooden wall beside them went up forever, and feet the size of cars thudded along the vast plain of the path. Annie cried out and clung on while Ned cantered toward the dark space beneath the shed's floor. The black soles of Jamie's sneakers rose above them, smacking down to miss them by a hairbreadth.

Ned swung around and together they peered out. More giant feet arrived and Annie recognized Dad's boots.

"Which way did she go, Jamie?" Dad's voice boomed out.

"I don't know. But I bet she's chasing after Penelope Potter on Pebbles. She's only got to hear a horse and she's gone."

"She was very rude running off like that in the middle of lunch. Still, while I'm out here I'll pull those carrots for Mrs. Plumley. Get me a bag, will you?"

The feet clumped slowly away in different directions.

"Sounds like I'm in trouble," said Annie.

"And so's that rabbit!" nodded Ned.

"Have you seen him?"

"No, but I've seen what he's eaten. Four lettuces have been munched down to stumps, enough carrot tops have been eaten to feed a family of rabbits, and there are chewed peapods scattered everywhere."

As if to prove Ned's point, an outraged cry rose from the vegetable patch as Dad discovered the damage.

"How do you know it was Floppy?"

"I found a hole in the fence with telltale hairs sticking to the wire. Something white and furry has squeezed through, all right."

"At least he's safe," said Annie. "Even if he is going to be the most unpopular rabbit in the universe when Dad finds out it was him."

Ned snorted. "And the fattest."

"Where should we look?" Annie asked. "We have to find him before he does any more damage."

"I've looked everywhere," said Ned. "Up the pole beans, around the beets, between the onions. You name it, I've been there."

"Maybe he's lying down somewhere," said Annie.

"I wouldn't be at all surprised."

"Or searching to find his nice cozy hutch."

"To do that, he would have had to squeeze back through the hole."

"Into Penelope's yard," added Annie.

They peeped out just as Dad's boots approached and disappeared above them, headed back into the shed. His feet on the planks were deafening, so it was a relief when he clomped outside again.

"He's going to dig up the carrots," said Annie, recognizing the pitchfork, its prongs as thick as planks, flying by above their heads.

"Let's go," said Ned. "The hole's at the other end of the garden."

He trotted onto the path while Annie kept a lookout for big feet. They cantered to the safety of the rhubarb and paused. A quick glance under the umbrella of leaves told them Floppy wasn't there.

Back on the path, Ned set off at a trot, but was soon galloping so fast that the wind whistled. It was miles to the other end of the garden, and Annie held on tight. They were tearing along at a terrifying rate,

when a missile the size of a tree trunk hurtled from the sky and landed in front of them. Annie ducked while Ned changed pace and jumped it. Another and another fell in quick succession, one behind them and one in front. Ned jumped the one in front, unbalancing Annie, who clung on until the end of the path, where they took shelter under some spinach leaves. "Someone's dropping trees," she said, thoroughly alarmed. Ned got his breath back as another orange missile joined the other on the path.

"Not trees — carrots," he said. "It's a pity there's no time for a nibble!"

He swung around and trotted on toward the hedge.

In front of them, a square wooden structure loomed as high as a skyscraper. Annie knew it was Dad's compost bin, full of grass cuttings and vegetable waste. Along the front, at ground level, was a place where one of the wooden slats had rotted, making a hole. Annie noticed it at once because, poking from it, testing the air, was a pink nose.

"Look," she whispered. Ned froze into stillness. They watched as a white head emerged, a white head with a pair of floppy ears. "It's him." The rabbit blinked sleepy eyes.

"Well, who'd have thought to look in the compost heap?" whispered Ned.

Just then, footsteps thumped toward them. Ned quickly retreated into the jungle of spinach leaves. The startled Floppy backed into his secret den just before black-booted legs stopped at the bin. Above them, Dad threw a fistful of chewed peapods onto the heap and raised the pitchfork. It flashed down, biting into the earth in front of Floppy's hole. The footsteps clumped away again, but the fork stayed put. Floppy was behind bars.

"Dad's trapped him," said Annie. "Without even knowing it."

"And a good thing, too," replied Ned.

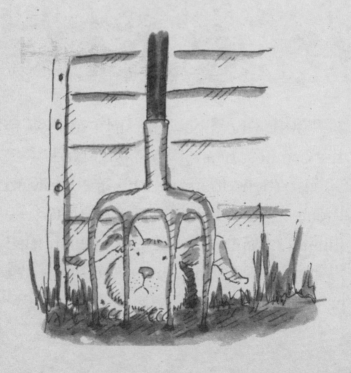

"All we need to do now is get you big again, and you can get him whenever you like."

Annie was overcome with delight. Floppy was found. She could hardly wait to tell Daisy.

But Floppy had no intention of remaining a prisoner. He urgently wanted to get out. He sniffed the prongs and tested all the gaps with his whiskers, but it was obvious he was too large to squeeze between any of them. With surprising determination, he scratched against a prong with his front paws, and when nothing happened, returned into the hole.

"He's caught, all right," said Ned. But when Floppy reappeared bottom first and heaved against the prongs with his back, Annie wondered if Ned was mistaken. At first nothing happened, then the fork slowly toppled.

"Look out!" cried Annie.

As quick as a flash, Ned jumped sideways and, for the second time that day, Annie landed halfway up his neck.

The fork boinged to the ground beside them. Floppy gave a satisfied twitch of his whiskers and hopped from his hiding place. He tested the air once more and set off purposefully in the direction of the cabbage row.

"That rabbit's going back for dessert," said Ned.

"I don't suppose he's ever heard of an angry gardener," said Annie, hauling herself back into the saddle. "We'd better go after him and quick, before he eats something else."

Chapter 5

The Magician's Hat

Annie had never been frightened of a
rabbit before, but then she had never met
one five times bigger than she was —
Floppy was at least the size of a rhinoceros.
As Ned closed the gap between them,
the hopping rabbit appeared to grow
larger. Annie couldn't think how to stop
him.

"We have to get you back to your normal size in order to catch Floppy," said Ned. "We'll go behind the pole beans. Hold tight."

Ned cantered for the cover of the beans and pulled up, blowing.

"Time to get off," he said.

"What will you do?"

"I'll go back to my poster. You catch that rabbit before he gets into more trouble."

Annie swung herself to the ground.

"Thank you for everything, Ned. Will you keep my riding clothes safe?"

"Of course," said Ned. "There's lots more riding to come. Now, go and catch that bunny."

Annie gave Ned a brief hug.

"Good-bye," she said, and let go of the reins. At once, the wind bore her away. When she opened her eyes, she was her regular size again, and Ned had disappeared.

She peeped around the pole beans. Jamie was piling the carrots into a plastic bag, Floppy was inspecting a young

cabbage plant, and Dad was checking the remaining heads of lettuce. Fortunately, he didn't know there were only the peas between himself and the greedy rabbit thief.

Voices and the sound of the side gate opening distracted everyone, even Floppy. It was Penelope Potter and her cousin Daisy. Penelope looked fed up and Daisy wasn't far from tears. The two girls crossed the grass, stepping around Jamie's magician's hat and cloak, which lay in a

messy heap. A wonderful plan popped into Annie's head. She darted forward, scooped up the surprised rabbit before he took a single bite, and, hugging her prize, darted back to her hiding place behind the pole beans. Amazingly, no one noticed.

"Hello, Penelope," said Jamie. "Who's your friend?"

"My cousin Daisy."

"Hello," said Daisy.

"Isn't Annie with you?" asked Jamie. "We thought you were off riding Pebbles."

"Fat chance! No, we're not riding Pebbles, and we haven't seen Annie for ages," said Penelope sniffily. Daisy pulled anxiously at the thin red leash she was carrying.

"We've been looking everywhere for Floppy," she said.

Dad straightened up. "And who may I ask is Floppy?"

"My pet rabbit."

"Your pet what?!"

Daisy looked up with wide, startled eyes. It was an awkward moment, saved by Annie, who jumped out from her hiding place.

"Hello, Penelope. Hi, Daisy."

"Annie, where've you been?" asked Dad.

"Looking for Floppy." For some reason she was no longer wearing her sweatshirt.

"I keep telling Daisy it's pointless," said Penelope. "If we haven't found him by now, the fox has surely eaten him. They love rabbits, especially juicy ones who are too fat to run away."

Daisy's face crumpled and she took a deep breath. "NO!" she wailed. "STOP SAYING THAT!"

The noise brought Mom hurrying to

find out what was wrong, and everyone gathered around the unhappy little girl.

"Oh, Daisy, be quiet," said Penelope, embarrassed by all the fuss. "You've got to face facts. We can't find him, and that's probably why."

In the noisy confusion, Annie reached behind the beans and gently lifted a

bundle from the ground before scampering across the grass to collect Jamie's magician's hat and cloak. Hands full, she hurried to the shed and scampered inside. Then she poked her head around the door and shouted above the din.

"Jamie! Come here a minute."

Daisy's cries lessened, and everyone turned to look.

"What for?"

"Something strange has happened to your magician's hat." Jamie turned to the place where he had last seen it. The fact that it was gone sent him racing.

"What's happened to it?"

"This," said Annie, and pulled him into the shed and closed the door.

From inside the shed came a lot of whispering.

Dad looked at Mom and raised an eyebrow. He started toward the shed but stopped in his tracks when the door burst open and Annie jumped out, tootling a fanfare.

"Taa taddle, ta, ta, taddle, ta, taaaaaa!

Ladies and gentlemen. Step up, step up to see the great magician Jamie and his magic hat." Annie clapped as loud as she could. The audience looked surprised and, in Daisy's case, astonished.

With a swirl and a flourish, Jamie stepped from the shed. From under the black cloak he took out his magician's hat and his magic wand.

"Abracadabra, dee diddle dabbit." He waved the wand and tossed it to Annie.

"From out of my magic hat comes . . . A WHITE RABBIT!"

Triumphant, he lifted out one bemused white bunny. In the pause that followed, Daisy's expression changed from misery to joy.

"FLOPPY!" she cried, and rushed forward. Jamie placed the rabbit in her outstretched arms, and the little girl

nuzzled her face in Floppy's fur, covering him with her curls.

"Well, blow me down," said Dad. "The thief in the garden, I presume!"

"Thank goodness for that," said Penelope. "Now we can go riding at last." She beamed at Jamie. "It was awfully smart of you to find him."

"I didn't," said Jamie. "It was Annie. I just did the thing I always wanted to do, which is to pull a rabbit out of my hat. Excellent!"

Later, when all the excitement had died down and Daisy had introduced Floppy to everyone, even Dad, Annie climbed the stairs to her bedroom. The first thing she saw was Tabitha, still fast asleep on the bed. She turned to the poster on the wall. Ned gazed out in the direction of the window, without doubt a poster pony again. Annie ran her fingers over the shiny paper and hoped no one

would notice that he was not in quite the same position as before.

She lay on the bed and put her arms around Tabitha, stroking the cat's soft nose and fluffy head. Tabitha half opened her eyes and purred.

"I've had an amazing adventure," Annie whispered.

Then she smiled up at Ned. "And I wish more than anything for another one soon!"